NICANOR'S GATE

KAR-BEN PUBLISHING®
An imprint of Lerner Publishing Group, Inc.
241 First Avenue North
Minneapolis, MN 55401 USA

Website address: www.karben.com

Main body text set in Adrianna Condensed
Typeface provided by Chank

Library of Congress Cataloging-in-Publication Data

Names: Kimmel, Eric A., author. | Massari, Alida, illustrator.
Title: Nicanor's gate / Eric A. Kimmel ; illustrated by Alida Massari.
Description: Minneapolis : Kar-Ben Publishing , [2020] | Audience: Ages 4–8. | Audience: Grades K–1. | Summary: A prosperous but simple and pious Jew of ancient Alexandria comes to the realization of why God has permitted his great wealth to accumulate.
Identifiers: LCCN 2019042915 (print) | LCCN 2019042916 (ebook) | ISBN 9781541574526 (library binding) | ISBN 9781541574533 (paperback) | ISBN 9781541599529 (ebook)
Subjects: LCSH: Nicanor, active 1st century B.C.—Juvenile fiction. | CYAC: Nicanor, 1st cent. B.C.—Fiction. | Jews—Egypt—Fiction.
Classification: LCC PZ7.K5648 Ni 2020 (print) | LCC PZ7.K5648 (ebook) | DDC [E]—dc23

LC record available at https://lccn.loc.gov/2019042915
LC ebook record available at https://lccn.loc.gov/2019042916

Manufactured in the United States of America
1-46592-47599-10/14/2019

Nicanor's Gate

Eric A. Kimmel

illustrated by Alida Massari

KAR-BEN
PUBLISHING

Long ago, in the days of King Herod, a man named Nicanor lived in the port city of Alexandria.

Nicanor was a merchant. His ships and caravans traveled the world from the tip of Spain to the Horn of Africa, bringing back jewels, gold, ivory, and spices.

Nicanor's wealth was beyond measure. Even Caesar himself, the emperor of Rome, once said, "Would that the gods favored me as they favor Nicanor."

But despite his riches, Nicanor was not a happy man. He often thought, "I have palaces at my command. Yet God's House is a ruin."

The beautiful Temple of King Solomon had been destroyed ages before. It had been rebuilt, but only enough to allow the priests to perform their duties. The broken stones, the charred walls, and the leaking roof were a sad reminder of the glory that once had been.

One day a messenger arrived with a letter for Nicanor. It came from King Herod himself. The king had decided to completely rebuild the Temple. He wanted to make it a proper place of worship instead of a patched-up ruin.

He invited Jews all over the world, rich and poor, to contribute to the building of the Temple.

Nicanor's heart leaped with joy as he read
the letter. Now he knew why he had been blessed
with riches. He wrote back to King Herod at once,
saying that he himself would provide the Eastern Gate,
one of the gates of the Temple.

Nicanor set to work. He hired the finest artisans in Alexandria to create the special doors. They were cast from Corinthian gold, a rare mixture of copper, gold, and silver that gleamed like the sun.

Making the doors took months. At last they were ready. Workmen loaded the doors onto specially built carts. The doors' weight would have crushed ordinary wagons. Teams of fifty oxen pulled each cart through the city.

Jews, Greeks, Egyptians, and Romans cheered as the doors rolled by.
Where but in Alexandria could such marvelous doors have been created?

The oxen pulled the doors to the waterfront. Nicanor directed the workmen as they loaded the doors onto the ship that would carry them to the Holy Land.

Wind filled the sails. Nicanor waved to his friends onshore as the ship left the harbor. He gazed at the city one last time. He would never return to Alexandria, he decided. He would spend his last years in the Holy Land.

After several days, the ship came in sight of Caesarea, the gateway to the Holy Land. "I am almost there," Nicanor told himself. "Tomorrow I will arrive in Israel. I shall walk in the footsteps of Joshua, David, and Solomon."

Lost in thought, he did not notice the sky darkening. The wind picked up. Towering waves crashed across the deck.

"Row!" the captain cried to the sailors. "We will be safe if we can reach the port."

But it was no use. The waves rose higher and higher. The howling wind carried away the mast.

"We must lighten the ship. Otherwise, we will sink!" the captain shouted. He ordered the sailors to cut the ropes holding the great golden doors.

"No!" Nicanor screamed. It was too late. The sailors pushed the uppermost door into the ocean.

"The other one too!" the captain cried.

Nicanor threw himself on top of the remaining door. "Throw me into the sea with it," he said. "My life is in those doors. If they are lost, so am I."

The sailors looked to the captain. What should they do? In that moment the wind died down. The sea calmed. The storm passed. The ship—and one of the doors—was saved.

King Herod met the ship at the port. He and his courtiers marveled as the sailors unloaded the remaining door. Its artistry was magnificent. It shined so brightly in the sun that their eyes hurt to look at it.

Nicanor could not rejoice. "My hope is at the bottom of the sea," he told the king. "What good is one door?"

"One door is better than no doors," said King Herod. "We do what we can. The rest is in God's hands."

Suddenly, a cry arose from the seashore. There it was—that immense shining door, so heavy that fifty oxen could hardly pull it—floating like a leaf on the surface of the waves.

King Herod's men dragged the door from the water and set both doors on the carts that were to bring them to Jerusalem.

With the doors in place, King Herod decreed that from then on, the Eastern Gate of the Temple would be known as the **Gate of Nicanor**.

In later years, the bronze and copper doors of the Temple gates were replaced with doors of gold. But Nicanor's doors were not touched. Not only were they the most beautiful, but a miracle had sent them.

When Nicanor died, the people of Jerusalem placed his bones in a stone box. They set it in a cave where the most honored people were buried. On it they carved these words:

Bones of Nicanor the Alexandrian,
who made the gate.